Bryce is a rabbit shifter recently kicked out of his nest because he's gay. Not the best way to start a life on his own, especially when he's caught and brought to an animal shelter. He supposes it's better than becoming rabbit stew, but still. He wants to be free.

Then in comes the boy.

Jess' son Taylor wants a pet, and for some reason, he picks the angriest rabbit Jess has ever seen. Jess isn't sure it's a good idea, but they bring Thumper home, and the rabbit settles down.

Then Jess wakes up to find a naked stranger standing in his living room.

Hopping to Happiness
Copyright © 2020 Catherine Lievens
ISBN: 978-1-4874-2864-8
Cover art by Angela Waters

Published by eXtasy Books Inc or
Devine Destinies, an imprint of eXtasy Books Inc

Look for us online at:
www.eXtasybooks.com or www.devinedestinies.com

Hopping to Happiness

By

Catherine Lievens

CHAPTER ONE

"So? What do you have in mind?" the woman asked.

Jess looked down at Taylor. "I'm not sure. I don't think you're ready for a dog just yet. Maybe a cat?" He wanted his son to have a pet, but he wasn't looking forward to having to take out a dog every day, multiple times a day. He didn't have it in him.

Taylor shook his head. "No." He paused and frowned. "I like cats. I just don't think I want one."

Please, don't say you want a dog. "What do you want, then?"

Taylor was still looking at the cages. He looked uncomfortable, and Jess couldn't deny he felt the same way. Maybe coming to the pet store hadn't been a good idea. It had been the most obvious one, but Jess was already starting to regret it.

He didn't like the thought of *buying* a pet. He was sure it was okay for some people, but he didn't want to buy a life. He didn't want to buy one of those puppies that would no doubt find a home easily. Maybe he should have suggested going to the shelter, but this was the first time he'd ever got a pet, and he hadn't even thought about it.

He was now, but he wasn't sure how to bring it up, especially in front of the lady who was trying to sell them a pet.

He crouched next to Taylor. "Not a cat, then. That's fine. Do you see anything else you might want?"

Taylor was still frowning. If it had been up to Jess, his eight-year-old son would never frown. He would always have a smile on his face because he would always be happy.

It was stupid, but Taylor was the light of Jess' days.

1

Taylor shook his head. "I don't like any of these."

Jess breathed easier. They were cats and dogs, but he'd seen Taylor look at the rodents, and even though they felt different from, say, the dogs, he still wasn't comfortable with buying one. He was wondering if there was a shelter for rodents, though. Were those abandoned? He didn't know, but he should look into that.

He rose from his crouch and patted his son's shoulder, then looked apologetically at the lady. "I'm sorry. We probably should have talked about this before coming. But we'll be back." That was a lie, but he didn't want to tell her there was no way he was buying a pet. He was the one who'd walked in there, after all.

She nodded, not looking disappointed at all. "That's okay. Buying a pet is a commitment. You should be sure of what you're doing before you do it."

At least she wasn't trying to get them to buy something, *anything*, just because she wanted to make money. Jess smiled at her, feeling slightly better. "You're right. It is. And while we *have* talked about it, it's obvious we need to have a longer chat. Thank you."

Jess steered Taylor out of the pet store and toward the ice cream parlor. He bought Taylor's favorite flavors—strawberry and lemon—and together, they sat on the bench outside, watching the pet store.

"It was a bit sad," Taylor said.

Jess smiled at how dirty his son already was. He was eight, but he still couldn't eat ice cream without slobbering all over himself. "What was sad?"

Taylor shrugged. "I don't know. All those puppies and kittens. I want all of them to have a home, you know?"

"But not ours."

"I don't think I want a cat or a dog. Those rabbits were cute, though."

Rabbits. Of course. "You're right, they were." Jess had no idea where to start with a rabbit, but he would learn.

Taylor hesitated. "We don't have to get a pet if you don't want one, Dad. I know they're a lot of work. I promise to do as much as I can, but you know I forget."

That much was true. Jess was convinced that if Taylor's head weren't attached to his shoulders, he would forget it every day. "We can talk about it again, sure. But you want a pet, and I think it's time. You're eight years old, and you're old enough to have your responsibilities and stick to them. It won't be easy in the beginning, and I'll make sure that whatever pet you choose always has food and water, but he'll be your responsibility." Taylor *really* wanted a pet, and Jess didn't want to say no, and Taylor seemed to understand there was a lot more to wanting a pet than buying one. "But if you don't think you're ready, we can wait."

Taylor shook his head. "I'm ready. I've been thinking about this, and I couldn't believe it when you said okay. But I don't want to take one here." He paused and cocked his head, still looking at the store. "But I think I might want a rabbit."

Jess took his phone out. "Let me see if I can find a shelter that also has rabbits, okay?"

Taylor's eyes went wide. "They have shelters for rabbits?"

"I don't know. We're about to find out, I guess."

He opened the browser and typed a few words in, holding his breath as his phone came up with results.

"Well, it looks like a few shelters in the area do have rabbits," he told Taylor after a moment.

Taylor's eyes widened, and he finally smiled. "When can we go?"

Jess checked the time. "Not today. I know I promised you we would start looking into it today, and we did. We came here. And if you want a rabbit, we can probably start to buy a cage, things like that." Although again, Jess needed to look into it more. "But I thought you would pick a cat or a dog, so I'm not prepared for rabbits. How about we take a few days to research what we're going to need if we get a rabbit, and then we go to the shelters?"

Taylor gave his ice cream a lick, then bit his lower lip. "Do you think Mom would have been okay with a rabbit?"

Jess sighed. Taylor's mother had died a while back in a car accident, and both of them still felt the loss keenly. Most days, Taylor was a normal eight-year-old boy, but sometimes, just like now, his mother's absence slithered into their lives. "She loved animals," Jess told him. "She probably would have brought home one of each."

That startled a laugh out of Taylor. "You mean one rabbit, one cat, and one dog?"

"She would have brought the entire *shelter* home if she could have." And she would be so proud of how Taylor was taking his time to think about this.

They'd been planning to get a pet once Taylor was a bit older, but she would never see it happen.

Jess pushed the thoughts away. He didn't like to think about Sandra. He loved her, but now the only memories he could focus on were of the night she died. He didn't want to think about her that way, though. "Let's go home. You can use your tablet to research what's needed for rabbits, and we can talk about it. Okay?"

Taylor nodded, then went back to his ice cream.

Jess breathed easier.

He knew he should talk to Taylor about his mom, and he was planning to. They did, sometimes, like today. But it still hurt, even after three years, and Jess wasn't sure he would ever get over it. He wasn't sure he was meant to. He knew some people thought he should start thinking about finding someone else, and maybe they weren't wrong. But this was easier. It was easier to focus on Taylor, on their life together, and not on dating.

That was something Jess wasn't ready for at all.

Bryce peeked around the dumpster, and once he was sure no one was in the alley, he hopped out. He sniffed, but the only thing he could smell was trash. It stank, and he wrinkled his nose.

He'd thought that hiding behind the restaurant would help him find food, but from the looks of it, he was going to have to shift. He didn't want to. He was vulnerable as a rabbit, but it would be even worse as a naked human. God knew what people would think of him if they saw him. Probably that he was a pervert, walking around naked in the hopes of finding someone.

That wouldn't do. He might be hungry, but he wasn't about to become a sex offender because of that. Maybe he could wait until it was dark to shift and go through the trash. He wasn't sure he would find something he could eat, but it was better than not looking at all. He was hungry. He needed food. Besides, in his rabbit form, he could survive on vegetables. It wouldn't be good for long, but for a while, it would be enough.

He sighed and went back under the dumpster. He wished he could still be home right now. He wanted to go back, but that would only happen if he told his alpha that he wasn't gay, maybe that he'd seen the light.

Bryce snorted. *Seen the light. Right.* Because that was how things worked. He knew damn well it wasn't, but he supposed he could fool his alpha if he tried. The fact was that he didn't want to, though.

Bryce was gay. *Very* gay. He'd only ever gotten hard for guys, and that wasn't going to change anytime soon. He should have known better than trying to date, though. He should have known better than to think his alpha would be accepting. He'd been riding on the high that his own family didn't care when he'd decided to come out publicly.

It hadn't gone well.

Bryce's family might not care about who he fucked, but his alpha certainly did. He'd given Bryce an ultimatum—either Bryce became straight and married a woman, or he got kicked out of the nest.

And kicked out Bryce had been.

He wasn't even angry at his family for not standing up for him. He understood. They needed the support the nest could give them, the work, the money, the food. It was hard to be a shifter out here, especially with humans not knowing about them. They had to hide if they wanted to be their true selves, and humans didn't usually understand why they lived all together. They thought they were cults, and while that wasn't true, it certainly felt like it right now.

It was because of the nest that Bryce wouldn't have his family anymore. It was because of the nest, or rather, the alpha, that Bryce was homeless and going through the trash to eat.

He sighed, then sneezed because of the stink. *Dammit.* He needed to stop thinking about what he'd left behind. He'd made his choice. It wasn't going to change, no matter how much he wished it would. He wasn't ever going to become straight, so this was his life now.

Bryce knew he would make it, eventually. He was a good person. He would find work and earn enough to get an apartment. It was these first few steps that were the hardest, and his stomach didn't like being empty. He supposed he should be grateful. Maybe like this, he would finally lose a few pounds. Alpha Johnson had always told him he could use it.

He stuck his head out from under the dumpster again and looked around. Staying here wasn't useful. Even if he waited until later to go through the trash, the evening was still a few hours away. The days were slowly becoming longer as spring advanced, so he would have to be careful.

But there was a park nearby. Bryce didn't like eating grass—it made him feel too much like a cow, which he definitely wasn't, even though he'd always been overweight—but it would do in a pinch, since he was so hungry. And bonus—grass didn't have a lot of calories.

He hopped out, moving slowly to be sure no one would notice him. He didn't think people would care if they found a rabbit hopping around, but you never knew. Someone might take pity on him and take him home, which would be a good thing if he could be sure of what would happen to him once he got there. He'd heard enough horror stories, though. It was the kind of stuff shifter parents told her kids at night so they'd be careful around humans, and since Bryce didn't fancy becoming rabbit stew, he was going to stick to what he knew and stay away from people.

He made it to the park. He wasn't sure how much time had passed, and he didn't care. He was a rabbit. Time was of no consequence for him.

He hid under a bush and started munching on grass, wrinkling his nose at the taste. He didn't like it, but his stomach was grumbling, and he needed to fill it. Maybe Alpha Johnson had been right. Maybe Bryce *should* have been a cow shifter.

Bryce shook his head. *No.* He needed to stop thinking about the alpha. The man had kicked him out for something Bryce couldn't change and didn't want to change. Bryce was gay, and he was proud of it. Well, he supposed he should say that he was proud of it as much as anyone could be proud of their sexuality. It wasn't like straight people went around saying they were proud of liking the other sex. But Bryce had never thought this was a problem for him. It didn't feel like it was. He didn't feel weird or unnatural. He felt like *Bryce,* and that was it. He didn't want to change only because some people thought he was wrong. Besides, if it wasn't the gay thing, it would be something else. Alpha Johnson had always had a problem with Bryce. In the beginning, it was just that Bryce was fat. Now, it was this. That was never going to change, and Bryce had had enough.

Still, he should probably have waited to come out until he had money set aside. Instead, he found himself in the middle of the street without even a pair of jeans to call his own. Luckily for him, it was spring, but still, the nights were cold.

"Look at how pretty you are," a voice cooed.

Bryce froze. He slowly turned his head and found a lady standing over him. He tried to hop away, but she was fast, somehow faster than he was. She snatched him from the ground and raised him to her chest, and Bryce tried to bite her.

He didn't want to become rabbit stew, dammit.

"Oh, no, you don't. I know you don't want to come with me, but I promise everything will be okay. I'm going to give you food, and you'll be warm and safe."

Bryce wrinkled his nose. Was she telling the truth? She wouldn't have a reason to lie to him, since she didn't know he was a shifter, but could he trust her? He supposed that no one would tell a rabbit they were planning to eat that he was about to become stew, but still.

He kicked, trying to push his way out of her arms, but even though she was elderly, she was damn strong. She didn't let go. Instead, she walked away from the park and toward a car. Bryce knew there was no way he would make it out if he got into that car, but he didn't have a say about it. He was just a rabbit shifter. Even if he bit her, she probably wouldn't let him go. She'd decided she needed to save him, and that was what she was going to do.

His eyes widened when she opened the back of the car and

saw a box inside. She gently put him inside, and he tried to hop out, but she was already closing the box.

This wasn't good. Not good at all.

Bryce had no idea what was happening when the car started to move. He didn't know where he was going or what was going to happen to him. It was terrifying, and he didn't know what to do about it. No matter how hard he tried to push the box sideways, it wasn't budging, and neither was he.

He had no idea how long it had been when the car finally stopped. He held his breath, listening to the sounds of the lady turning the car off, stepping out, and walking around to get him. He was ready to fight as soon as he was out of the box, but of course, instead of taking him out, the lady picked up the entire box and walked away with it.

Great. Bryce was sure he'd make for a damn fine rabbit stew, but he still hoped she'd choke on it.

CHAPTER TWO

"Ready?" Jess asked Taylor.

Taylor was staring at the building in front of them. He nodded, and Jess knew they wouldn't leave this place without a pet.

He wasn't sure he quite liked the idea.

He hadn't changed his mind, though. He wanted Taylor to have a pet, to understand the responsibilities that went with that. Besides, Taylor was still focused on a rabbit, even though Jess didn't understand why. Rabbits didn't make as much of a mess as dogs did, and they weren't as big assholes as cats were. Or at least, Jess hoped they weren't.

He and Taylor had spent the day researching rabbits and visiting the pet store again. In their living room now stood the biggest cage Jess had ever seen. It was odd, and it took a lot of space, but he wasn't about to put it in Taylor's bedroom as Taylor had suggested.

"Do you think we'll find him today?" Taylor asked.

"Him?"

Taylor shrugged. "I don't know. I thought it would be nice for me to have a boy rabbit."

"So we're only looking at boy rabbits today?"

"I guess not."

That was good, because Jess didn't know how many rabbits the shelter had. He'd called earlier to make sure that they had at least one, and they did. Jess hoped that Taylor would like that rabbit and wouldn't force him to drag him around to other shelters to find his perfect pet. He didn't know if rabbits

10

had their own personalities like cats and dogs, but he suspected that was the case with most animals, and that meant that they needed to be lucky if they wanted to find the perfect one.

He gestured at the shelter. "Well? Let's go."

He knew Taylor was nervous, but he wasn't surprised that he wasn't saying anything about it. That was his son—ever since he'd lost his mother, he thought he needed to be strong for his dad. It was ridiculous, but it still made Jess a little proud.

They walked into the shelter, and the man at the front counter looked up. He smiled at them and leaned over the counter. "Good morning. I'm Mark. What can I do for you?"

Jess rubbed the back of his neck. "I called earlier. We'd like to see your rabbits, please."

Mark's eyes widened. "Of course. I remember you. Not a lot of people want to adopt rabbits."

"Well, we do." Jess was grateful for this guy and the work he did, but he wanted to go home. That wouldn't happen if they didn't have a rabbit, so the sooner they got it, the sooner they would leave.

"Follow me," Mark said. He left his spot behind the counter and headed toward the back door. Jess gently pushed Taylor that way, then followed his son.

The place smelled. It wasn't bad, but it was odd, and nothing he was used to. He supposed that with as many animals as there were here, he shouldn't be surprised. He hoped their rabbit wouldn't smell like this, though. He wasn't sure he could deal with having this kind of smell in his house all the time.

"As I already told you on the phone," Mark said. "We don't have many rabbits, just a few. We did get a new one yesterday, though, and hopefully, he'll find a home with you. Of course, you should take your time and get to know the rabbits individually. They all have their own personality, just like humans, and you might find that one is more like what you expected than the others. There's nothing wrong with that, just like there's nothing wrong in saying that none of the rabbits we have is the pet you're looking for. It's important to us that every pet we give away finds a good family."

Jess already knew he was going to have to fill out forms, and that was fine with him. Anything to make Taylor happy.

Mark stopped in front of a door. "Here you go. The rabbits are in here."

To Jess' surprise, it wasn't another room they stepped into, but a small backyard. There was a patch of grass with an enclosure around it. There was a door, and inside, several wooden huts.

A furry nose popped out of one of the huts, and the rest of the rabbit followed. This one was white, and the only thing Jess could think of was how easy it would be to get the rabbit dirty. He wasn't looking forward to giving the rabbit a bath.

Mark crouched next to the railing and stuck a finger through it. The rabbit hopped closer and stuck his nose against it, and Mark laughed. "Rabbits are cute. I don't understand why people only want dogs and cats."

"I want a rabbit," Taylor exclaimed. He crouched next to the man and stuck his finger in, too.

Jess held his breath. He knew that with a rabbit, Taylor was no doubt going to get bitten at least a few times. Jess was going to have to deal with tears and possibly a little blood. He'd warned Taylor that it would happen, but that hadn't changed Taylor's mind.

Jess looked around. This was a shelter, and while he'd never visited one, he'd imagined what it would look like. It was nothing like that, though. Everything was clean and neat, and he felt better about the place.

"This one is Melissa," the man said. "She's very nice and

sweet. She likes carrots. Do you want to feed her one?"

Taylor agreed, but Jess could see that he wasn't convinced about Melissa. She was a cute rabbit, but clearly, Taylor hadn't fallen in love with her.

Jess listened as Mark pointed out a few of the rabbits. None of them made Taylor smile, though, and Jess had resigned himself of having to go to another shelter when Taylor pointed at the back of the enclosure. "What about that one?" he asked.

"This is our newest arrival. Like I told you, he was found yesterday. He was in the park. Someone probably left him there thinking he would be able to make it, since there's grass and everything." The man wrinkled his nose. "Rabbits don't just eat grass." His gaze turned to Jess. "I'm sure you're aware of that?"

Jess nodded. "I've done some research, and we'll take the rabbit to the vet, of course. We're doing this the right way." He couldn't look away from the rabbit Taylor had pointed at. It had to be the angriest looking rabbit Jess had ever seen. It looked like it might eat anyone who came too close, and that included Taylor. Jess wasn't sure how comfortable he was with having his son close to that beast.

"Do you want to get closer?" Mark asked.

Jess almost said no, but it looked like they were taking this rabbit home, so he supposed he should get used to the idea.

He watched Taylor step into the enclosure and walk closer to the angry rabbit. The other rabbits hopped around, careful, but the angry one stood its ground. It was weird. Jess thought it would have run away, but instead, it was trying to stare them down.

Taylor crouched in front of it and held a finger out. "Hi. My name is Taylor. Do you want to come home with me and my dad?"

Jess smiled. Of course Taylor would ask the rabbit for its

permission to be taken home.

"Why this one?" Mark asked.

"Because he's angry. I'm sure he's scared and that he wants to go home."

Jess melted a little. He might not be convinced about the rabbit, but if this little guy was the one Taylor wanted, then he was the one who would go home with them, no matter what Jess thought about it. He wasn't the one making decisions in this case. Taylor was, and Taylor always made his decisions with his heart.

Bryce was pissed.

He'd thought he was going to become food when that lady had picked him up at the park yesterday, but instead, he'd been washed, poked, and put in an enclosure with other rabbits.

Real rabbits. Rabbits who couldn't shift into a person. Rabbits who didn't understand anything.

So yes, Bryce was angry.

He glared at the little boy crouching in front of him. He realized he was lucky he hadn't been neutered or something like that. Was that even a thing with pet rabbits? Nothing had been done to him, not even vaccines. But he knew that if anyone adopted him, that would be his future.

He was not a real rabbit, for fuck's sake. He didn't need a family. He didn't need to be adopted. He didn't want either of those things.

But it looked like he was going to, willing or not.

The man who'd dragged him around to the vet and back yesterday reached for him, and Bryce resisted the urge to bite him. "Are you sure you want this one?" the man asked. "He's not very sociable."

"I want to give him a reason to smile." The little boy

frowned. "Do rabbits smile?"

Bryce resisted the urge to roll his eyes. He wanted to, but real rabbits didn't do that.

"I don't think so," the other man said. From the way he behaved, Bryce thought he was the little boy's father. "But if you're sure you want this one, it's fine with me."

"I do. I want him to be happy. I think I can do that. What do you think?"

"You can make anything happen if you want to."

Bryce *really* was going to roll his eyes eventually, and someone would realize he wasn't a real rabbit.

He wasn't a father, so maybe it was just that he didn't understand, but those two were so sweet they were making his teeth rot, and that was never a good thing when you were a rabbit.

Bryce supposed he should be happy that he was leaving the shelter, especially this soon. The people who were adopting him looked like they were nice, too, which was a plus. Bryce didn't think he would end up in a pan, so that was good. Still, he needed to find a way out. He'd been stuck in the shelter, and now he was probably going to be stuck in a cage somewhere. He couldn't shift in a cage, not unless he wanted to hurt his human body, and that wouldn't do. He was homeless. He needed to be at least healthy.

The bad, bad man who'd taken Bryce to the vet yesterday took him inside. He directed the boy and his father to sit in the waiting room, then took Bryce away. Bryce had to resist not biting him — again. He wanted to, but he realized that this guy had nothing to do with his situation. He and the lady who'd found him were trying to help. If Bryce had been a rabbit, he probably would have been relieved to have a place where he could be warm, safe, and have as much food as he wanted. This would be a rabbit's heaven. Instead, Bryce was bitching because he wanted to be free.

But maybe being adopted wasn't going to be that bad. Yes, Bryce would be in a cage, but it would give him a few days to recuperate. Life on the streets was hard, and he wasn't used to it. He didn't *want* to get used to it, but he knew better than to hope. So he knew that eventually, he would go right back to it, but in the meantime, maybe he could take a week or two to eat and rest. That could only be useful for when he went back.

He did his best not to glare at the little boy once the man carried him to the waiting room in an open box. He wasn't sure why the boy had chosen him, and he wasn't sure he believed what the boy had said about making Bryce happy. Surely no one was that nice? None of Bryce's siblings had been, even the young ones. Maybe that had more to do with Bryce than with them, though. As far as Bryce knew, maybe everyone in the nest hated him. No one had raised a finger when he'd been kicked out, that was for sure.

"Here you go. He saw the vet yesterday, and he's healthy, but I suggest you make an appointment anyway," the man said as he handed the box to the new man. There were holes in it, but Bryce still hated not being able to see what was happening out there. He'd have to jump to see through the holes, and he didn't want to do that in case he ended up on the floor.

"We will. Thank you," the man said. His voice was soft, gentle, and it made Bryce shiver. He wasn't sure it was a good thing. He didn't want to find out.

"Good. You have everything you'll need for the rabbit?"

"I think we do. We did a little research yesterday after Taylor decided he wanted a rabbit. We went to the pet store earlier this morning and bought the biggest cage they had, as well as everything else."

"Good. The vet will be more precise when it comes to the rabbit's diet, but here's the list of things he can and can't have, and what he's been eating since yesterday. You shouldn't give him too much to eat, or he'll become fat. He's already over-weight as it is."

Bryce scowled at the top of the box and threw himself against one of the sides. The man yelped, but unluckily for Bryce, he didn't drop the box. Still, that would teach him to be rude.

"Here you go. Better you than me."

Taylor's father chuckled, but there was a hint of fear in his voice as he took the box. The rude man closed it, and Bryce was in the dark. Those few holes didn't help, unfortunately, and Bryce e didn't like the dark. "Thank you again."

"I hope I'll never see you again," the man said.

"I'm sorry?"

"You know. Because it will mean that you haven't aban-doned the rabbit."

Bryce *did* roll his eyes this time since no one could see him. What the fuck was this guy thinking? Did he think he was endearing? Or was he trying to seduce the father?

Bryce frowned. Was that it? He was gay, but since he'd had to hide it, he didn't have a lot of experience with guys. Maybe this guy was just trying to be nice. Or maybe he was trying to get laid, who knew?

Bryce could feel Taylor's father walk away, and he prayed that whatever was waiting for him outside the box wasn't go-ing to be horrible. Since there was a kid involved, he sus-pected that Taylor's father wasn't lying. He probably really just wanted a pet for his kid, and that was good.

Bryce wasn't sure how much time had passed, but he knew he'd been in a car, and now he was out of it. He could feel the box move. Then someone put it on the floor. Bryce held his breath, then blinked when the box was opened and flooded with light. Taylor's face appeared, along with his father's.

"What now, Dad?"

"Now, I'm going to put him in his new cage. You know

Catherine Lievens

what the website said. We have to give him a few days to get used to our presence, so no cuddling him yet."

Taylor looked very serious as he nodded, and Bryce's heart did a weird flip-flop. This kid looked like he cared what happened to him. He wasn't the kind of kid who would pull on Bryce's ears or play with him like a doll.

Bryce let Taylor's father pick him up. He didn't move, didn't try to bite, and he could see the relief on the man's face. He was gently put into a cage, then it was closed, and Bryce was in prison again.

It could have been worse—that much was sure. It could also have been much, much better, though. Bryce was going to have to find a way out of this, and he didn't know how. He didn't even know where to start.

Taylor sat next to the cage cross-legged and peered inside. "This is your new home. I'm Taylor, and my dad's name is Jess. I hope you're going to be happy here."

God, the kid was too sweet for his own good. At least now Bryce knew their names. If he had to live with these two people, he needed to know their names.

But where was the mom? Bryce hadn't seen her, and Taylor hadn't mentioned her. Did that mean she wasn't in the picture? From the sound of it, no one else lived here other Taylor and his father, and it made Bryce wonder.

He shouldn't. He should want to be out of here as soon as possible. He should want to find a way out.

Instead, he settled down on the straw and listened to Taylor talk to him about his life and how happy they were going to be together.

CHAPTER THREE

That rabbit was weird. Jess wasn't sure *what* was weird about it exactly, but he knew it was.

It kept on watching Jess and Taylor. Jess wasn't sure it was normal behavior for a rabbit, but he supposed they were lucky the rabbit didn't look like it was going to kill them in their sleep anymore. He didn't look happy, either, but what did a happy rabbit look like anyway?

Jess peered out of the kitchen door to the cage in the living room. The rabbit was sitting there, staring. Jess moved back to the counter and cut another tomato.

He should have thought better about getting a pet. He'd thought Taylor would want a cat or a dog, but instead, they found themselves with that carrot-eater. It wouldn't be so bad if the rabbit wasn't so freaking weird. Of course, Jess had never owned a rabbit, so maybe this was entirely normal.

"Dad! I think I found a name for him!"

Jess couldn't help but smile at the sound of Taylor running closer. He turned around as Taylor burst into the kitchen. "Really? Is it better than White?" he teased.

Taylor glared. "It was a good name, like the rabbit from Alice in Wonderland."

"I know. But White is kind of, well, boring."

"That's why I found another name for him."

"All right, I'm listening." Jess put down the knife. "What's his name?"

"Thumper."

Jess pressed his lips together. "Thumper?"

"Yes. Like the rabbit in Bambi."

"I know who Thumper is. You're right. It's cute." And Jess suspected that the rabbit was going to want to kill them again once it heard that, even though it made zero sense. "Why don't you go tell him?"

Taylor's smile grew. "You're right. I can see if he likes it. I'm not sure what I call him if he doesn't, but I still have to tell him."

Taylor ran away — did that kid ever walk like a normal person? Jess turned back to his tomatoes. He supposed he should feel lucky that Taylor hadn't picked Roger as a name for the rabbit. He didn't think Taylor knew the movie, thank God.

He listened to Taylor as he settled next to the cage. "Hey, Mr. Rabbit. I have a new name for you. You have to tell me if you like it or not, okay?"

There was a pause, and Jess imagined that Taylor was waiting for the rabbit to nod or something. "Okay. What do you think of Thumper? It's not as boring as White, but still a famous rabbit name."

Jess couldn't help it — he peeked out of the kitchen to make sure the rabbit wasn't nodding at Taylor — or trying to bite him to death. At this point, he wouldn't be surprised if that was exactly what was happening.

But it wasn't. The rabbit was still sitting there, staring. He didn't look like he wanted to kill Taylor, which was a good thing, but he didn't look happy either.

Taylor wiggled his fingers through into the cage. "So? What do you think?"

"It looks like he likes it," Jess said.

He could have sworn the rabbit turned his head toward him and that its glare deepened.

Jess swallowed. He half expected the rabbit to try to kill him in his sleep.

"I don't know. He doesn't look happy," Taylor said.

"Well, he's only been here a day. Maybe he still needs to get used to us. Why don't you go wash your hands? It's nearly time for dinner."

Taylor jumped to his feet and ran to the bathroom, and Jess put his knife down again. He grabbed one of the carrots he'd cut and walked to the cage, where he crouched in front of the rabbit. He stuck the carrot between the bars, then peered at the rabbit. "So. Thumper, huh? I hope you like it, because I'm pretty sure it's going to be your name."

The rabbit's eyes narrowed, and Jess would have taken a step back if the rabbit had been a person. Luckily for him, he wasn't.

Jess rose from his crouch and patted the cage. "Well, Thumper, *bon appétit*."

Dinner, like always, was a whirlwind of telling Taylor to stop talking and eat and listening to him. Jess had gotten used to the fact that he could barely get a word in the conversation a long time ago, and he was more than happy to let Taylor drone on about whatever new game he'd invented or movie he'd watched. As long as Taylor ate, Jess didn't have a problem with it. He wasn't a talker anyway.

Once they were done, he sent Taylor to take a bath while he cleaned the kitchen. Periodically, he peered into the living room because he heard something. He wasn't surprised to see the carrot was half gone, but he *was* surprised to see the rabbit was in its usual spot, staring again.

That rabbit was fucking weird, and Taylor had better have picked the right one, because Jess wasn't going through this again. *Are all rabbits like this?*

"Come on, Taylor. Hurry up," Jess yelled a few times to keep Taylor moving. He'd stop doing what he had to do if Jess didn't remind him of it every so often.

It always took Taylor a while to finally get to bed, but once he was, he fell asleep almost right away. Jess went to flop onto the couch in front of the TV and sucked in a breath. Finally, he could relax.

He reached for the book he'd abandoned on the coffee table and put his feet up, then settled in to read, but it wasn't long before his eyes started sliding shut.

He shook his head a few times. He didn't like this. He never had time to do what he liked. Between his job, Taylor, and the house, he always reached nine PM exhausted. He didn't have time for what he liked and what he wanted to do, but he supposed it wasn't going to change anytime soon. He didn't regret raising Taylor on his own. He could have accepted his mother's suggestion that she moved in with them, but he hadn't wanted to, and he still didn't. He and Taylor were a family, and they needed to stand up as one.

Still, most days, he keenly felt the loss of a second parent. He felt the loss of his *wife*, even though three years had passed. He and Taylor seemed to be getting on nicely, but days like these, Jess still found himself turning to ask his wife what she thought about something—in this case, about Thumper.

Jess peered at the rabbit, who was nowhere to be seen and had hopefully finally gone to sleep. He felt better not being stared at, but he knew that wasn't going to last long.

He sighed and started to read his book again. He wanted to get to the end of this chapter before he went to bed. He might not be able to read as much as he used to, but he could read at least a few pages before heading upstairs.

Jess was asleep, and this was Bryce's chance to make it out of here.

He'd noticed that Taylor hadn't closed the cage well when he'd opened it to clean it earlier today. Bryce could make it out, then shift and leave before anyone noticed.

He felt a pang of sadness at the thought of Taylor discovering that his pet rabbit was gone the next morning. He didn't want to hurt the boy. He'd been nothing but nice to Bryce, even though to him, Bryce was nothing more than an animal. But this had to be done. Even though Bryce was comfortable, fed, and warm, he *wasn't* a pet rabbit. He was a human, and he needed to live as one.

He waited a bit longer to make sure Jess wouldn't wake up. Jess was cute. The book he'd been reading had fallen on his stomach while his head was tilted to the side. He had to be uncomfortable with his neck twisted that way, but from what Bryce had seen, he doubted Jess would wake up. He had to be exhausted.

Bryce still hadn't seen a mother, so he suspected there wasn't one. He didn't know why, and it didn't matter. What *did* matter was that he'd watched Jess take care of the house and his son all alone, and he was impressed, even though he hadn't been here long. If things had been different, if Bryce had been human when he'd met Jess, if Jess was bisexual, Bryce could have so easily fallen in love with him. Jess was a good man, and even though Bryce had only been with them one day, the thought of leaving made him ache.

Taylor and Jess were a family — a family Bryce didn't have anymore.

He shook his head. Even though his first instinct was to stay, he couldn't. He took a second to gather himself, then he pushed the side opening open and held his breath when Jess murmured something. Jess didn't wake up, though, so Bryce hopped out of the cage, wincing at the sound the opening made when it fell back. He held his breath, but Jess was truly asleep. He wouldn't wake up, and Bryce forced himself not to be disappointed. He shouldn't be.

Bryce shifted. It had only been a few days since he'd last been human, but God, he needed this. He stretched, then looked around for a blanket or something he could use to cover his body. He was going to have to find clothes, and he wasn't sure where or how. There was no way he could fit in Jess' clothes. Jess was taller and thinner, and his clothes would probably explode if Bryce tried to put them on.

Bryce turned around, headed toward the kitchen, wondering where the laundry room was. Maybe he could steal a sheet or something like that. He needed to find clothes that he could wear. Not having been human when he'd been kicked out meant that he had nothing—no clothes, no money to buy clothes, no cell phone. Nothing.

He wasn't about to steal anything more than a sheet from Jess and Taylor, though. They'd been so nice to him. He wouldn't thank them for what they'd done that way.

"What the fuck?"

Bryce squeaked and turned around, his hands flying to cover his groin. Jess was awake, sitting up on the couch, his eyes wide as he stared at Bryce.

Shit.

Jess had no idea what was happening. A naked man was standing in the middle of his living room, and he didn't know how that man had gotten there, who he was, or what he wanted.

Jess reached to the side and grabbed one of the pillows, then threw it at the guy. The guy raised his hands to protect his face. "I'm sorry! Please, I'm not here to hurt you!"

Jess didn't listen. He grabbed another pillow, got to his feet, and slammed it against the man. The man stumbled back, even though Jess couldn't have hurt him.

"I promise I have an explanation," he yelled between two blows.

"An *explanation*?" How was he supposed to explain that he was naked in Jess' living room? And with Taylor upstairs sleeping? Was this guy a pervert? Where the fuck were his clothes?

Jess held the pillow up again, then slammed it against the side of the man's face.

The man stumbled and raised a hand to catch himself against the wall, and Jess reached for his phone on the coffee table. He already had the nine and one dialed when he turned around to make sure the guy wasn't about to attack him.

The man was gone.

Jess blinked. He looked around, his finger poised to hit the last one and dial if he needed to, but as far as he could see, the man was gone. He didn't know where, but he didn't relax.

He lowered his phone, putting it into his pocket just in case he needed it later. There was no way the guy could have left without Jess noticing, which made Jess wonder where he was. He couldn't have gone upstairs—Jess would have seen him, and he would have stopped him however he had to.

Something squeaked, and Jess jumped. His heart was racing, and he expected the man to jump up from somewhere when he realized that it was Thumper and not a naked serial killer.

But Thumper wasn't in his cage anymore.

Jess frowned and took a cautious step toward the area where he'd heard the squeak come from. It was right where the guy had disappeared, and it didn't make sense, although of course, nothing seemed to be making sense right now.

Thumper was sitting on the floor, his head cocked, his ears drooping. Jess make sure the man wasn't there before crouching next to Thumper. "What are you doing out of your cage, Thump?"

The rabbit wrinkled his nose. He didn't answer, of course, but he hopped toward Jess.

Jess reached out to take him, but instead of coming closer, Thumper decided to hide under the couch. Jess swore and tried to catch the rabbit before he disappeared under there, but he couldn't. Thumper was faster than he was.

Jess straightened, still swearing. "What the fuck? What's going on? Am I dreaming?" He'd fallen asleep while reading, so he supposed it as possible. Strange, but possible.

But the guy had seemed so real, and Jess was sure he'd hit him with the pillows. *No.* He'd been real, even though he was nowhere to be seen.

Jess raked a hand through his hair. What was he supposed to do now? He couldn't go to sleep, not knowing there might be a guy wandering around the house entirely naked. He couldn't call the police because he didn't have anything to show them.

"I'm sorry."

Jess jumped, his heart *exploding* out of his chest, or at least, that was what it felt like. He twirled around, and there was the man, half-hidden behind the couch.

The man raised his hands, and now that Jess was less freaked out—albeit not by much—he could see that the man didn't look dangerous or threatening. That didn't mean Jess trusted anything he was saying, though.

"I promise I'm not here to hurt you," the man said.

Jess looked around for a better weapon than his pillows. He didn't care why the man was here. He wanted him to get out of his house, and he wanted that to happen *now.*

He took his phone out of his pocket while grabbing yet another pillow, but when he turned around to throw it at the guy's head, he was gone again.

Jess flopped onto the couch, unable to understand what was happening. What was the guy? Where had he gone again? There was no way could have disappeared that fast if he was human, but of course, he had to be. Only humans existed, right?

Or maybe he was a ghost. Jess didn't know what to think

anymore. He'd never believed in ghosts or paranormal stuff, but maybe he should start.

He didn't know what to think, and he didn't know what to do. The man was gone, but was he still inside the house? And what did he want? There was no way Jess could go to sleep before finding him. He wouldn't put Taylor in danger. He had to do something.

But what?

Bryce didn't know what to do. He'd fucked things up, and now he had to fix them.

But how?

There was no way Jess would listen to him. Bryce had already tried talking to him twice, and every time, Jess hit him with those pillows. It didn't hurt, but it wasn't comfortable either, especially not on naked skin. That was why Bryce had shifted, and he was going to continue doing that until Jess calmed down and was ready to listen to him.

He wiggled back under the couch and dragged himself to the other side. Jess sat there, and Bryce could too easily imagine what he was doing. Freaking out, as he ought to. This situation would be funny if Bryce weren't so desperate to make Jess understand. It was frustrating.

Bryce never intended for this to happen, and he didn't know how to fix it. He was supposed to be out of the house before Jess woke up. No one was supposed to find out what had happened. Jess and Taylor would have woken up tomorrow morning, and they would have found Thumper gone, and it would have been sad, but they would have gone on.

And Bryce would have been out there, afraid to go anywhere, roaming the city and starving to death.

Bryce was in trouble, and he wasn't used to getting himself out of it on his own. He'd always had the nest and his family at his back, but no more. He was alone, and he had to solve his problems on his own.

He peered out, wondering if Jess had calmed down. He didn't want to freak Jess out even more, but he wasn't sure what else he could do. He needed to explain to Jess what had happened.

A big hand wrapped around him and pulled him from under the couch. He squeaked and tried to get away, but Jess held him against his chest.

"I don't know what's happening, Thumper, but I don't like this," Jess said. He pressed a kiss to the top of Bryce's head, and Bryce allowed himself to close his eyes for a second.

He wished he could have this all the time, but in his human form. He wanted a family. He wanted a place where he could belong, and he knew he would never find that again. The only place where he'd belonged had been the nest, and they didn't want him. They'd kicked him out, and now, he was alone.

Jess stroked his fingers down Bryce's back. "Maybe I was dreaming. What you think, Thumper? Was it a dream? The guy felt real, but how am I supposed to know? He's not even here anymore. I can't call the cops and tell them there's a disappearing naked man in my living room. They'll laugh in my face." He rubbed his fingertips under Bryce's chin. "What should I do?"

Bryce wanted to tell him that he needed to put him down and listen to him, but of course, he couldn't. He also couldn't allow Jess to put him back into the cage, though. This was his chance to escape. He wasn't sure he wanted to anymore, but he also couldn't stay here.

When Jess rose from the couch, Bryce knew he needed to make a decision. He needed to do something unless he wanted to be put back into the cage. Who knew when he'd have an opportunity like this one again? Maybe never. If Jess realized the cage had been left open, he would make sure it was closed every night, and Bryce would be stuck in there.

Bryce kicked, and when Jess didn't release him, he bit down on one of Jess' fingers.

That did the trick. Jess yelped and loosened his hold, and Bryce managed to jump out of his hands. The problem happened when Jess tried to catch him on his way down. He almost managed, but Bryce was too fast. He ended up falling right on his face, pain exploding as he shifted back without meaning to.

And here he was, in his human form, ass up and face down as if he were begging for Jess to fuck him, completely exposed to his gaze.

This was ridiculous. He *wasn't* waiting for Jess to fuck him. It might look that way, but it wasn't his fault he'd fallen on his face.

He rolled to his back and tried to hide his groin from Jess' gaze. He wasn't sure there was anything he could do for the rest of his body, though. Jess was peering down at him, his eyes wide, his face paler than it had been before, his mouth opened.

Bryce prayed he wasn't about to start screaming.

CHAPTER FOUR

Jess needed to sit down.

He reached out with his arm, and his knees were wobbly. The couch was close by, but it felt too far away. Jess wasn't sure he'd make it there, and he needed to before he fainted in front of this guy.

This naked guy who just went from being a rabbit to, well, a naked guy.

"What the fuck?" Jess muttered as he finally found the couch. He sat onto it hard and tried to breathe in and out before he went full-blown panic attack. He would be justified to do just that, but he didn't want to wake Taylor upstairs.

Taylor. He would freak out just as much as Jess was if he found out what had happened, or if he came downstairs to find his father with a naked man he didn't know. Jess needed to stay quiet, no matter how much he wanted to scream.

The man scrambled into a sitting position. He was trying very hard to cover himself, and Jess took pity on him. He reached out and grabbed the blanket that was draped over the back of the couch, then threw it at the naked man. "You can have that."

The man took it with a grateful smile. "Thank you."

Jess nodded. He wasn't sure he knew what to say to that.

He wanted answers, but he didn't know what kind of questions to ask. He didn't know up from down right now. Had the guy *really* gone from being a rabbit to a human being? It only happened in books. This was impossible. Jess had to be dreaming.

He blinked. Maybe he'd never woken up after falling asleep while reading. Maybe he *was* dreaming. He allowed himself to feel hopeful for a second, but he knew he was only trying to fool himself. Of course he wasn't dreaming. He was awake, and he'd really seen what he'd seen, no matter how weird it was.

The man crouched next to Jess, and Jess turned his attention to him again. He'd wrapped the blanket around his body, hiding everything he needed to hide. He looked worried, as if he cared what Jess was going through, and Jess found himself blinking at him, not understanding.

"Are you okay?" the man asked.

Jess laughed. "How can I be okay? I just saw you transforming into a human being." He paused. "That means you can also become a rabbit. *Our* rabbit."

The man chuckled nervously and rubbed the back of his neck. "You're right. I'm Thumper."

Jess giggled. He knew he was freaking out and that he was becoming hysterical, and he needed to stop before it was too late. He slapped a hand on his mouth and stared at the man with wide eyes.

The man sighed. "I should leave."

He was right. He *should* leave. No matter what kind of explanation he gave Jess, Jess didn't think it would help. He didn't know if this guy was a wererabbit or something else, and he didn't know if he wanted to find out. Ignorance was bliss, and he wanted to bask in that for a moment, or possibly for the rest of his life.

But could he? He'd seen what he'd seen, and there was no denying that. There was no erasing his memory. Even if he managed to convince himself it had all been a dream, there was a part of himself that would always know that wasn't the case.

He rubbed his face. He wanted to go to bed and forget all

about this, but he couldn't, not when there was a naked rabbit man in his living room.

What was next, then?

Bryce didn't think he'd ever been in this situation. He'd lived with shifters his entire life, so he'd never had to be there when a human found out about them. He didn't think he'd ever had any human friends, come to think of it.

But Jess was freaking out.

Bryce knew he should leave. His first instinct was to go to the door and abandon Jess, but he couldn't. Jess and his son had taken Bryce in, even though they hadn't known he was a shifter. They'd kept him safe, warm, and fed. They had compassion for small creatures they thought didn't matter, or rather, a lot of people thought didn't matter. Bryce *had* mattered to them, though, and he wanted to repay that, although he wasn't sure he could.

The least he could do was take care of Jess while he freaked out. He could only imagine what would happen if he left right now, and that didn't sit right with him. He didn't know if Jess was afraid of him, but that was certainly a possibility. He would have to face it if Jess showed signs that he was afraid.

Jess was in shock. Bryce wanted to help.

He looked around. The blanket wrapped around him threatened to fall at any second, and it was uncomfortable to have so much free movement around his groin, but he didn't want to give it up. He was grateful for the second blanket that was draped over the armchair and reached out to grab it, pulling it closer and wrapping it around Jess' shoulders. He cautiously sat next to Jess, keeping a safe distance between them just in case Jess freaked out at his presence. So far, Jess hadn't reacted aggressively, but what was to say he wouldn't eventually? Bryce wished he had more experience with things like this, but he didn't, and he had to play in the dark.

"I'm a rabbit shifter," he began. There was no hiding what he was from Jess, not anymore. Jess had seen him shift. He probably thought it was all a dream right now, but eventually, he'd realize that wasn't the case. When that happened, he would either freak out even more or accept what was happening. It might be easier if Bryce explained.

Jess blinked at him. "Rabbit shifter?"

"You know, like in the books. Although in books, shifters are usually wolves or bears, or something big and powerful like that. I'm just a rabbit."

"Just a rabbit."

Yep. Jess was still in shock. "I'm Bryce, by the way. Not that I don't like Thumper, but Bryce is my real name. My human one."

Jess blinked again. "Bryce. And you're a rabbit shifter."

"I am. That's how I was able to turn from a rabbit to a human being. I'm not planning to hurt you. I promise. I'm grateful for what you did by adopting me."

That seemed to do the trick. Jess shook himself, and his gaze became more focused. He narrowed his eyes. "Why were you in the shelter in the first place?"

"Not on purpose, trust me." Bryce swallowed. He didn't know if telling Jess his story was the right thing to do, but he doubted he could get out of this if he didn't. "A lady picked me up at the park the other day. She thought someone had abandoned their pet rabbit. I could have shifted and left, but I couldn't allow anyone to find out what I was."

"But I did."

"By accident. I didn't think you were going to wake up when I tried leaving. If I had a choice, you wouldn't have found out. Not because I don't want you to know," Bryce added in a rush. "But because humans tend to freak out when they realize shifters are real."

Jess snorted. "That's an understatement." He rubbed his face. He looked tired, but Bryce suspected he wouldn't go to bed until he had all the answers he wanted. Bryce was more than happy to give them to him if Jess asked him questions. "Why were you in the park in the first place? Were you having a nice lunch munching on grass or something?"

Bryce shrugged and looked away. He knew he shouldn't be ashamed of what had happened to him. He'd been kicked out by the people who should have protected him. The only reason he was living on the streets was that they hadn't allowed him to take anything with him.

Still, he didn't want to admit that he was homeless. He felt like a failure, and he hated it. But he owed Jess the truth. "My family kicked me out recently. They did so in my rabbit form, so I wasn't able to bring anything with me, not even clothes." Bryce gestured at his body. "Which is why I'm naked, by the way. Shifting doesn't carry clothes from one form to the other, so even if I'd been human and dressed, I would have ended up naked when I shifted back from my rabbit form. But anyway. What I'm trying to say is thank you. And I hope I didn't freak you out too much, although I know I did."

"I don't understand any of this."

"I'm sorry. I'll leave right away." That was what Bryce had been trying to do anyway. "I never meant to scare you. So thank you for what you did, even though you didn't know I was a guy." He started to stand up, but to his surprise, Jess' hand shot out in front of him. Jess didn't touch him, but it was evident that he wanted Bryce to sit down again.

Bryce obeyed. Even if he did need to leave, he wasn't looking forward to it. He'd only meant to do that because he didn't want to live his life as a rabbit in a cage. He was also part human, and he needed that part to have just as much time in his life as the rabbit one. Living as a pet rabbit wouldn't have achieved that.

But now that Jess knew, Bryce wasn't looking forward to having to go back on the streets, especially as a rabbit.

"You were a rabbit the entire time, right?" Jess asked.

Bryce nodded. "I was. I never shifted inside your house before. I couldn't do it in the cage because I didn't want to hurt myself."

"But Taylor took you out yesterday."

Bryce couldn't help but smile. "I didn't think you knew about that."

Jess rolled his eyes. "I know everything that happens in this house. I wasn't surprised he didn't obey when I told him to leave you in your cage for a few days. You're his first pet." Jess wrinkled his nose. "But anyway. I know he took you out yesterday. Why didn't you shift then?"

Bryce looked down at his hands. "I couldn't. I would have scared Taylor."

"And that's why you haven't shifted? Because you don't want to scare my son?"

"Of course I don't want to scare him. I didn't mean to end up here, but once I did, I never wanted to hurt you or your son. I just wanted a warm home and food, and that's what I got. But I know I can't stay here indefinitely. It just doesn't work like that."

"So you're planning to go back on the streets?"

"Well, since I don't have a home, yes."

"That doesn't seem right."

"That doesn't matter. It's what I have to do. I don't have a home. My parents, or rather, my nest, kicked me out. They're not a home for me anymore. I don't have anyone else, so it's either stay as a rabbit for the rest of my life or go out there and live on the streets." Bryce didn't want Jess to pity him, but he also didn't want to lie. This was how things were, and there was no changing it.

"I can tell there's a story there," Jess said.

35

"There is." But Bryce didn't want to talk about why he'd been kicked out, just in case Jess decided to side with the alpha. "I promise I wasn't kicked out because I was dangerous. They just found out something about me they didn't like."

Jess' eyes narrowed, but to Bryce's relief, he didn't ask what Bryce was talking about. "And you don't have anyone else? You could go to a shelter."

Bryce shrugged. "I'm sure I could, but do you think they would take me in? I'm entirely naked. They'd probably think I was nuts or something, and they would take me to the hospital."

Jess tapped his fingertips on his thigh. "I see." He seemed to make a decision, and Bryce held his breath. He already knew he needed to leave, but *how* he was going to leave came down to Jess.

"You can stay here."

Bryce blinked. "I'm sorry?"

"You can stay here for a while, at least until you find a job and put enough money away to get an apartment."

Bryce gaped. He couldn't believe what he was hearing—he didn't understand it.

But he wasn't going to look a gift horse in the mouth.

Jess would probably regret this eventually. He didn't know what he was doing, and he realized he must be crazy, letting a stranger stay in the guest room.

But he couldn't kick Bryce out, not after he'd heard the man's story.

Anyone else probably would have. Even though Bryce seemed like a sweet man and was as cute as a button, he might still be a serial killer waiting for his chance to hurt Jess and Taylor. But he *hadn't* hurt them. Even when Taylor had let him out of his cage yesterday, he'd stayed in his rabbit form because he hadn't wanted to scare Taylor. Someone who wanted to hurt them would have shifted. Jess had been in the house, but he couldn't have done anything about it.

Instead, Bryce had stayed in his rabbit form. He'd allowed Taylor to play with him and cuddle him. And all that because he hadn't wanted to scare Taylor. Jess thought that said a lot about him and what he wanted to do with his life, and Jess hoped he could help him.

Bryce hadn't told him why he'd been kicked out, and Jess didn't want to imagine the reason behind it, but whatever it was, it probably wasn't fair. Bryce looked like he couldn't hurt a fly, neither in his rabbit form nor in his human one. Why would his parents, or rather, his nest as he'd called it, kick him out? Why would they want him to live on the streets? No one should be homeless, and while Jess still thought that going to a shelter might be a good idea, he understood where Bryce was coming from and why he didn't want to.

So apparently, he was going to say in Jess' guest room.

Jess rose from the couch and rubbed his face. "You can stay here," he repeated.

"Thank you. You don't have to do that, though. I know you decided to take in a pet rabbit, and that you feel responsible for it, but I'm *not* a pet. I can survive on my own."

Jess didn't snort, but it was a close thing. Sure, Bryce would probably survive on his own for a bit, but for how long? He'd been caught once already, and he'd been lucky he'd ended up in the animal shelter rather than somewhere else. He probably wouldn't be as lucky a second time.

And Jess would never be able to forgive himself if something happened to Bryce when he could have stopped it by letting Bryce stay in his home.

Yes, it was dangerous. He might even regret it eventually. But he also would regret not offering, and that wasn't something he wanted to deal with.

He stopped in front of Bryce. "I know I'm not responsible for you. I'm just trying to be helpful. I don't know why you got kicked out, and I don't want to know." That was a lie, but Jess wouldn't demand an answer. "You don't have to tell me. I'm offering my guest room without any reservations or conditions. There are just a few rules. I don't want you to tell Taylor about this, not yet. He can't know that shifters exist." If Jess couldn't wrap his mind around it, he couldn't imagine how Taylor would react. "And you can't hurt him or me."

Bryce frowned. "I already told you I wasn't planning on hurting you. I know it's probably hard to believe me considering everything, but if you think I'm dangerous, then I'll go."

Jess shook his head. "You can stay. I'm not changing my mind. But you can't deny that all of this is hard to wrap your mind around. I don't know what to make of it."

Bryce rose, too. "Look, Jess, thank you for letting me stay here, but you don't have to if you don't feel comfortable with it. I know that you don't want me to be homeless again, but unfortunately, that's not going to change anytime soon. I need to find a job, and finding one without clothes is impossible. I don't want to steal. It might come to that, and eventually, I'll probably do it. But again, none of that is your business. So thank you for offering me a place to stay, but since you're uncomfortable with it, I'm going to go."

Bryce was right. It was true that Jess was uncomfortable, but he still couldn't allow Bryce to leave.

Bryce didn't look like he could defend himself from anyone. He was short, and there wasn't a single muscle on his body, not that Jess had seen. He was too trusting. Jess didn't have a problem imagining Bryce going with a stranger because they were offering him something, be it food or shelter, and something bad happening to him.

And something *would* happen. Jess didn't think of himself as a savior. But would helping Bryce be such a bad thing?

"I said you could stay here, and I'm not changing my mind. Come on. I'll show you to the guest room. You can take a shower since you probably need it, and in the meantime, I'll find you some sweatpants or something you can wear. They might not fit right, but at least you won't be naked." Jess frowned. "Should I get you some food, too?"

Bryce shook his head. "You fed me well when I was a rabbit. I'm a bit bored with carrots right now, but I can wait until tomorrow morning." Bryce hesitated. "Thank you. Not a lot of people would do what you're doing."

Jess realized he was probably saving Bryce's life, but it still made him uncomfortable to have Bryce thank him. "Don't mention it. You need help, and I can provide it. That's all I'm doing."

They both knew it was more than that, but thankfully, Bryce didn't bring it up as Jess showed him to the guest room. Jess didn't know how things would work out, especially tomorrow morning once Taylor was awake and he found a man he didn't know sleeping in the house while his pet rabbit was gone, but Jess would find a way.

There was always a way, and Jess knew that he and Taylor would get through this, too.

Chapter Five

Once again, Jess didn't know what to do. That seemed to be his entire life since he and Taylor had adopted Thumper — or rather, Bryce.

But Taylor was sad about his rabbit having disappeared, and Jess didn't know how to solve that. He didn't want Taylor to be sad. He wanted his son to be happy, but he knew that offering to pick up another rabbit wouldn't help. No, the only thing that would work would be to explain to him what had happened, and Jess wasn't sure that was a good idea.

Taylor was eight. He wasn't ready to face the fact that there were more than human beings out there. Or maybe it was just a problem Jess had. Jess was still trying to wrap his mind around Bryce's existence, even though it had been almost a week since it had happened.

But in that week, Bryce had acted like a normal human being. He was awkward and shy, and he tried to stay out of Jess and Taylor's way, but he was there. He was living with them, and Jess couldn't ignore that.

Jess had already had a hard time explaining to Taylor who Bryce was. He'd told his son they were friends, but Taylor hadn't quite believed it. He'd never met Bryce before. But Bryce was sweet and quiet, and he was good with Taylor. That had surprised Jess. He hadn't expected Bryce to fit so seamlessly with their family, but he had, and Jess couldn't deny that.

Taylor and Bryce had fun. Bryce made sure Taylor did his homework during the evening, and he'd picked up a lot of chores around the house, which meant that Jess was free to focus on reading or any other thing he'd been putting off because he didn't have the time.

It was like having a second parent in the house, even though Bryce wasn't Taylor's father. Jess felt slightly guilty about that, but he knew he shouldn't. He was finally able to sleep well, and as much as he needed. He could stop obsessing and worrying over giving Taylor everything he needed because Bryce was there to pick up the slack.

That probably shouldn't be as comforting as it was, but it was.

"You think he's okay?" Taylor asked in a tiny voice as Jess pulled up the blanket to cover him.

Jess sighed. "I'm sure Thumper is fine." He knew for a fact that he was, but he couldn't explain himself.

"Why you think he ran away?"

"Because he's an animal, love. He saw the cage was open, and he took his chance."

Taylor's eyes widened. "So it's my fault?"

Jess sighed again and sat on the bed next to his son. "I know that saying this isn't going to help, but I'm sure Thumper is okay and that you don't have to worry."

Taylor didn't look convinced, but what was Jess supposed to say to him? Maybe he should rethink having Bryce talk to Taylor. He wasn't looking forward to having Taylor find out about this new world that Jess was still trying to wrap his mind around, but maybe it was the right thing to do. Jess wanted Taylor to be prepared.

But Taylor was only eight. Could Jess really do that to him? He probably would have to if Bryce stayed in their lives, but everything was so uncertain right now that Jess didn't know what to do.

That seemed to be the way he felt about pretty much everything these days.

He leaned forward and kissed Taylor's forehead. "We'll talk about it tomorrow, okay? Try to get some sleep."

Taylor nodded, but Jess could tell he still had something to say, so he waited. Sure enough, after a moment, Taylor looked at him. "What about Bryce?"

Jess frowned. "What about him?"

"Is he going to stay here with us?"

Jess bit his lower lip. "Do you want him to?"

Taylor nodded, much more enthusiastically than Jess had expected. "I like him. He's nice."

That much was true. Jess hadn't been sure the first few days, but now he knew that Taylor and Bryce were good together. They weren't father and son, of course, but Bryce acted like an authority figure, but also like someone Taylor could talk to when he needed to. It hurt a bit not to be his son's only adult figure anymore, the one person he went to when he had something to talk about or when he was hurt, but Jess knew it was a good thing. Taylor needed to trust other people, people who weren't him, and Bryce was a good place to start.

"I don't know what's going to happen with Bryce," Jess said. "But for now, he's staying with us, so don't worry." Losing Bryce right after losing his rabbit would probably be too much for Taylor.

Maybe Jess hadn't made the right decision when he'd allowed Bryce to stay here, but he couldn't regret it, not even now.

Jess left Taylor in his bedroom to sleep and headed downstairs. He stepped into the kitchen, intent on cleaning up before going to bed, but he blinked when he saw that everything was already clean and neat. He wasn't surprised, though. Bryce had a tendency to do things without being asked. More than once, Jess had discovered that the chore he'd been planning to do had already been done.

Jess couldn't help but smile. He headed to the living room,

flopping onto the couch. Maybe he could finally finish his book tonight. He sure was going to try.

"What's wrong?" Bryce asked as he stepped into the living room, too. He was holding a basket full of folded laundry, and while Jess had a moment of uncertainty at the thought of Bryce folding his underwear, he couldn't bring himself to care.

"What makes you think something is wrong?"

Bryce cocked his head. Jess had insisted on buying him clothes that fit him, and he looked good enough to eat with his jeans and t-shirt. He was barefoot, too, and Jess liked how comfortable he was in the home. It was as if he'd always been here, as if he belonged with Jess and Taylor, and Jess was starting to think that maybe he did.

"You always have that frown when you're worried about something," Bryce said, putting down the laundry basket and gesturing to his forehead.

Jess touched his own. "I'm not frowning."

"Not anymore, but you were a few minutes ago." He hesitated. "Do you want to talk about it? Because you don't have to if you're not comfortable with me."

Jess supposed there was no better person to talk about whether or not he should let his son know that shifters were real. "I was wondering if I should talk to Taylor about shifters."

Bryce sat in the armchair. He leaned forward, intent on what Jess was saying, but he was far enough that he wasn't touching Jess. Jess had noticed that about him. He always made sure that both Jess and Taylor were comfortable with his presence and that he wasn't in their personal space.

Jess bounced his knee. He wasn't used to talking with others about how he raised Taylor. "I mean, I want him to be prepared, just in case he ever stumbles onto shifters. You're a rabbit shifter, but since you mentioned that there are other

43

species around, I want Taylor to know."

Bryce nodded. "You're right. I'm not dangerous, since I'm a rabbit, but some people shift into bears and other big animals, and *that* is dangerous."

Jess agreed. "But on the other hand, I don't want to throw his life into disarray. What's he going to say if I tell him shifters are real? How is he going to react?"

"You think he won't believe you."

"In part. I also don't want him to be burdened by all of this, though. He's so young."

"You're right, he is. He's only eight. But there are shifters out there who are children, and as far as you know, one of them might be in Taylor's class. It's not like you're telling him about serial killers, or about sex, or whatever. You would explain to him that while yes, most of the people around him are human beings, some of them might have a little something more than that." He bit his lower lip.

Jess couldn't help but stare. He wanted to pull Bryce's lip away from his teeth. He wanted to replace them with his own.

Jess blinked. When had he started looking at Bryce that way? Had he been attracted to him in the beginning? Jess couldn't remember, and he wasn't sure he would have noticed if that had been the case. He'd been so focused on the rabbit shifter thing that he'd barely noticed anything else about Bryce.

"I could show him," Bryce suggested. "I'm a rabbit shifter and his pet rabbit to boot. He probably won't be afraid of me if I show him I'm a shifter. But of course, you're the one making decisions in this case. I can only make suggestions. I'm ready to do it if you agree with it, though."

He wasn't wrong. He was a rabbit shifter, which meant he wasn't dangerous or intimidating. He was probably the perfect person to do this.

Jess was still hesitant when it came to explaining to Taylor that shifters were real, but he did want Taylor to be prepared if he ever stumbled onto one. He didn't want Taylor to freak out in an unknown environment. If Taylor had to panic, it might as well be here, with Jess around.

Jess nodded. "Let's do this."

Bryce hadn't expected Jess to want to do this now considering Taylor was already in bed, but to his surprise, Jess got up and headed upstairs. Bryce stayed where he was, bouncing his knee and wondering if this was the right thing to do.

He didn't have a say in the decision, of course. He was nothing to Taylor, while Jess was his father. But he'd volunteered to help make Taylor understand what being a shifter meant, to show him that shifters were real, and now, he couldn't help but wonder if Taylor would see him differently once he knew the truth.

Bryce shouldn't care. He hadn't known Jess and Taylor for long, just over a week. They were nothing to him, yet they felt a bit like the family he'd had to leave behind.

But they were different. Bryce's parents and his nest had accepted him because they'd had to, because he was blood — and because they hadn't known he was gay. Jess and Taylor were different. They didn't know Bryce. Jess should probably have kicked out Bryce the day he'd found him naked in his living room. No one would have blamed him for doing that, but he hadn't. Instead, he'd taken Bryce in, had given him a roof over his head, clothes, and food.

Bryce would never be able to thank him enough for that, and if explaining to Taylor what a shifter was like Jess wanted him to was a way to do that, he was more than happy to do it. He wished he could do more. Doing this didn't feel like nearly enough, but Bryce suspected that nothing would. Jess had given him a life, even though he might not even understand it or realize it. Bryce did, though.

"What's going on?" Bryce heard Taylor ask.

"Bryce and I just need to talk to you."

That was Jess, and the sound of his voice made swallowing hard.

He could do this. He'd never had to come out to anyone is a shifter before, except for Jess, and that hadn't gone the way it should have, but that didn't mean he couldn't do it. It was just words and maybe shifting in front of Taylor. Bryce hoped Taylor wouldn't be angry that his pet rabbit Thumper was Bryce. He hoped that realizing Thumper hadn't left and that he wasn't hurt would help.

Honestly, he had no idea what he was doing, and he had no idea how this would end.

Jess guided Taylor into the living room, and Bryce sat up straighter. He smiled at Taylor, but he knew that the smile was a nervous one. Taylor smiled back, looking confused. He sat on the couch where his father guided him, then looked from Jess to Bryce. "Why do you have to talk to me now?"

Jess settled next to him. "We have something important to tell you."

"Important?" Taylor blinked. "Are you two boyfriends?"

Bryce cocked his head. He wasn't touching that one with a ten-foot pole.

Jess made a strangled sound. "Why do you think that?"

Taylor shrugged. "I don't see why you shouldn't. Lisa has two dads."

Bryce knew Lisa was in Taylor's class, but he hadn't known about her to dads.

Jess cleared his throat. "Of course, but this is different."

"Why? You don't like Bryce? Maybe because he's not a woman like Mom?"

Jess shook his head. "I like Bryce." He snapped his mouth shut, and his eyes widened. "We're friends."

Taylor wrinkled his nose. "So he's not your boyfriend?"

"No."

"That's too bad. I thought he was, and I thought he was going to stay here with us."

Bryce's heart raced. Taylor wanted him to stay. Of course, that might change as soon as he found out who Bryce was, but in the meantime, the words made Bryce feel warm inside.

"I already told him he doesn't have to leave. That's not why we asked you to come, though. We have to talk to you about something. It will be a little hard to understand, but you're safe, and nothing is going to happen to you. I promise."

Taylor's eyes went wide, and Bryce couldn't help but wonder if Jess was going to this the right way. To him, it looked like he was scaring Taylor even more, and that couldn't be good.

Bryce didn't miss the way Jess looked at him, and he wasn't sure what it meant. Did Jess want him to go ahead and blurt out the truth? Was he thinking about Taylor's questions of them being boyfriends?

Bryce couldn't say he hadn't thought about it — because he had. How could he have not? He, Jess, and Taylor had settled into what was almost like a little family unit. Bryce didn't quite belong, but he'd made the house his, at least in some ways. He knew he was welcome everywhere. He contributed by doing chores, helping Taylor with his homework, cooking for the entire family, and washing the laundry. It made him feel less useless since he still didn't have a job.

But they weren't really a family, were they? Even if Jess liked him the way Taylor thought he did, that didn't mean he was going to act on that, and if he did, it didn't mean he wanted Bryce to keep living with them.

God, this situation was so freaking complicated, and Bryce wasn't sure what to do to make it simpler. It felt like anything he did would make things worse, so he kept his mouth shut and let Jess take the lead. It wasn't like he had any experience with this, be it with living with a kid or telling anyone he was a shifter.

So he looked at Jess, wanting to follow his lead.

And Jess looked right back at him.

Bryce huffed. "That's how it's going to go?" he asked.

Jess shrugged. "I figure you're the best person to tell him."

And that way, if he hated the news, he wouldn't be angry with his father. It made sense.

Bryce swallowed and looked at Taylor. "Okay. Just like your father said, no one is going to hurt you. I'm not danger-ous."

Taylor frowned. "I already know that."

"Good. Okay." Bryce was flustered, and he hoped he would make it out of the conversation without being a blub-bering mess. "See, there's something I have to tell you about me, about what I am." God, why was this so complicated? It shouldn't be.

But it was, and Bryce knew that it was because he cared more about Taylor than he should. He didn't want Taylor to hate him, or worse, to be afraid of him. He wanted to stay here and be a family with Jess and Taylor.

He had to look away from Taylor as he spoke. "What I'm trying to say, and what I'm making a mess of, obviously, is that I'm not entirely human. I'm a rabbit shifter. *Your* rabbit."

There was a pause, and considering how much Taylor usu-ally talked, Bryce was surprised not to hear a peep from him. He peered cautiously at the kid, only to find him staring at him. He couldn't say if Taylor was shocked, afraid, or some-thing else. He was just *staring*.

"Bryce can explain what that means," Jess said, not so help-fully.

Bryce glared at him.

But Jess was right that Taylor probably needed more

information. Bryce cleared his throat and looked at the kid again. "What I mean is that I can turn into a rabbit. I'm Thumper, the rabbit you brought home from the shelter. I never meant to lie to you or anything like that, but I couldn't stay in the cage. I can become a rabbit, but I'm also human, and I need to do human things, sometimes. I hope you understand that?"

Taylor finally blinked. "What does it mean that you can become a rabbit?"

Bryce had no idea how to explain that. "I just can."

"Is it magic?"

"I guess, in a way."

"How does it work?"

Trust the kid to ask hard questions. "I'm not sure. No one ever explained it to me. They didn't need to. I always knew how to do it. It's like there's a side inside me, something that's not exactly me, but that also is."

Taylor's frown deepened. "That doesn't make sense."

"It's just that I'm not sure how to explain. I never had to."

"Why don't you show him," Jess suggested.

Bryce glared again, but Jess might not be wrong on that, either. Maybe if Bryce showed Taylor, Taylor would understand better.

Bryce got to his feet and walked around the couch so he wouldn't give Jess and Taylor an eyeful of what was under his pants. "So I have to be naked to shift, mostly because otherwise, I'd be tangled in my clothes. I'm just going to take my jeans and underwear off, though. Jess, it won't be a problem for you to help me out of the t-shirt once I'm Thumper, right?"

"Of course not." Jess sounded hesitant, but at least he hadn't said no.

He quickly abandoned his clothes on the floor, then shifted. As soon as he was Thumper, Taylor's head appeared over the top of the couch. "You're a rabbit," he said.

Jess was right there with him, gently pulling Bryce out of the t-shirt. He raised him cautiously as if he was afraid Bryce was going to bite him.

Bryce seriously considered that possibility, then decided it was probably better not to do it.

"Can I touch you?" Taylor asked. Bryce nodded at him, and he closed his eyes when Taylor stroked the top of his head. "You're really Thumper."

That, Bryce was. And Taylor didn't seem to hate him for it, which was a great thing.

"Maybe you should shift back to your human for now," Jess said.

Bryce nodded again, and Jess put him down before him, and Taylor moved back to their seats. Bryce was shifting when he heard Taylor say, "But now I don't have a pet rabbit anymore. Can we get another? Please?"

Luckily for Bryce, he was still in his rabbit form, or he would have burst out laughing.

CHAPTER SIX

"Thank you," Jess said.

Bryce blinked up at him from the armchair. "What for?"

Jess realized it was probably stupid to thank Bryce for talking to Taylor days after it had happened, but he'd waited to see how Taylor took it.

It had gone well. Taylor had had quite a few questions, but Bryce had answered them as well as he could, and while Taylor hadn't talked to Jess about it until today, Jess had been keeping an eye on him. Then tonight, when he'd put Taylor to bed, Taylor had asked Jess to talk for a bit, and Jess had.

"For talking to Taylor. He just told me that he was excited about the fact that shifters exist."

Bryce smiled, and his entire face brightened. "He's not freaked out, then? That's good. I was afraid he would be angry or scared."

"Not at all. He sounded excited about you being a shifter. He seems to think it's the best thing in the world."

"Well, I'm happy everything went okay. But you don't have to thank me. I just told him what I am. Nothing more."

"But if you hadn't, *I* would have needed to have a chat with him, and God knows how that would have gone. I would probably have messed things up." Mostly because Jess didn't know much about shifters except that they could become animals. He should probably do a little research, but where should he start? It wasn't like he could *Google* it. There might be some stuff there, but it was probably related to books or crackpots. Bryce, on the other hand, *was* a shifter, and he was right there in Jess' living room.

"Well, thank you," Jess said again. "I'm pretty sure it would have been a disaster if you hadn't taken things in hand, and now it won't be because Taylor is okay with it."

"I was happy to do it. You've done so much for me, and it was the least I could do."

That wasn't true. Bryce did a lot around the house, even though Jess had never asked him to. He was looking for a job, and at the same time, he also took care of pretty much everything. Jess was coming back from work to find that the house was spotless and Taylor had already started in on his homework. He'd been able to stop hiring a babysitter when he came home late.

On the other hand, though, he kind of felt he was taking advantage of Bryce. Sure, he'd given Bryce a place to stay, and he was feeding him and everything else, but Bryce was working so hard. Jess wanted him to find a job — of course he did — but he already knew things would change once it happened. He didn't want to think about the moment when Bryce would leave. He didn't want Bryce to leave, period.

But he wasn't about to say that out loud.

"I'm also sorry for what Taylor said," he told Bryce instead.

Bryce frowned. "About what? I can't remember anything he said that offended me."

"Not offend, maybe, but he did think we were boyfriends."

To Jess's surprise, Bryce laughed. "And I should have been offended by that? Because I'm not." He hesitated. "I'm gay. That's the reason I was kicked out of my nest. The alpha didn't want me to be. He wanted me to be normal."

Jess didn't like where this conversation was going. "And I'm ready to bet that *normal* for him is straight?"

Bryce chuckled. "You got it. I came out to my family, and they took it pretty well, so I decided to come out to the rest of the nest. I thought they would be okay with it, you know?

They've always been my family."

"But instead, they kicked you out."

"It was more of an ultimatum. Either you find yourself a girlfriend and you can stay, or the door is right there, and you know how to use it."

"I'm sorry." And Jess really was. He'd never been kicked out by his parents, but he'd been through his fair share of hate. "I'm bisexual."

Bryce blinked. "Oh?"

"What I'm trying to say is that when I was in college, I had relationships with a few guys, as well as girls. I had to deal with homophobia and biphobia, too. Some people thought I was gay and trying to hide it. Some hated me because I dated guys. I'm not saying it's the same, but I can imagine all too well what you've been through, and I'm sorry."

Bryce shrugged. "It's in the past."

"A recent past, though." And that meant it still had to hurt.

"Yeah, but honestly, I was lucky. I can only imagine what would have happened to me if you hadn't offered me your guest room. I should be the one thanking you, not the other way around. You've done so much for me, and I don't think I'll ever be able to thank you enough."

Jess leaned closer and grabbed one of Bryce's hands, squeezing it. "If I don't have to thank you, then neither should you. I was happy to offer you my guest room, and I'm happy to have you here with us. And I wouldn't even care if you stopped doing the laundry or taking care of the house. I never expected you to do anything like that in the first place."

Bryce stared at their linked hands. "I know you never asked me, but it's the least I could do." He looked up at Jess. "You know, I wouldn't mind."

Jess wasn't sure what Bryce was talking about. "What wouldn't you mind?"

"I guess I'm just trying to say it wouldn't be so bad if you and I were together. That's all. I mean, about what Taylor said. He thought we were together."

Jess' eyes widened. Now he understood what Bryce was talking about, and he wasn't quite sure what to do with it.

He couldn't deny he'd thought about it. How could he have not? Bryce was there, always. He was in Jess' house, in the kitchen, in the bedrooms, in the living room. Even though he hadn't been here long, his presence was everywhere, and Jess realized that he'd settled down in a way that hadn't happened since his wife died.

It also felt like a betrayal, though. Yes, he liked Bryce, and he could easily imagine the three of them—Jess, Bryce, and Taylor—as a family. He knew it was stupid to feel like he was betraying Sandra, Taylor's mom. She would have been the first to want Jess to continue being happy after her death. She would have wanted Taylor to have another parental figure. She would have loved Bryce, and she would have loved the fact that he could become a rabbit.

So yes, Jess had thought about him and Bryce together. Bryce was adorable. He was the nicest person Jess had ever met, even after what had been done to him. He was gentle but firm with Taylor, and he was so, *so* loving, even though he did his best not to show it. It was in every gesture he made toward Jess and Taylor, though, so there was no hiding it.

Jess took his hand away from Bryce's and rubbed it on his thigh. "You wouldn't mind if we were boyfriends?"

Bryce's cheeks flushed, and he looked down again. "I wouldn't. But I understand why that's not possible. I mean, you just did me a favor. You're letting me stay here, but eventually, I'll find a job, and I'll have to leave. I'm going to miss this, though. Being with you and Taylor made me feel like I have a family again, and I'm going to hate losing it a second time."

That went straight to Jess' heart. He was hesitant, both

because of personal reasons, like how he felt when it came to having a new relationship with anyone, but also because he couldn't be sure Bryce wanted something with him because it would be convenient or for other reasons. Bryce wasn't taking advantage of him, but maybe falling into a relationship with him sounded good because it was too easy. Bryce would have a place to stay, even when he found a job, and Jess would have someone else, someone who could help him with the house and Taylor.

But no. That wasn't the only reason Jess wanted Bryce. He wanted Bryce because he was a gorgeous human being, and Jess could see himself fall in love with him so easily, even though he had conflicting feelings about it.

Bryce wasn't sure where this was going, but he liked it. He wasn't the one who had to make a decision, here, though. Jess was. Bryce already knew what he wanted.

He wanted Jess. He wanted Jess and Taylor.

He was just a guest, or at least he was for now. But what Jess was saying could mean a lot to him, and he was nervous. He didn't want to force Jess into something he wasn't ready for. Jess had told him about Taylor's mother, and Bryce knew how much both he and Taylor still loved her. They always would, and that was fine with him. He never wanted them to stop loving a woman that had been so important to them. He didn't feel threatened by her.

But she might be the reason Jess wasn't ready to be with him.

Bryce had thought about this, of course. Even before Taylor had asked them if they were boyfriends, he hadn't been able to avoid noticing how the three of them had meshed together. The only thing missing was him and Jess being together. For the rest, they kind of already were a family. Jess went to work, and since Bryce didn't have a job yet, he took care of the house and Taylor as much as he could. He knew that even when he found a job — if Jess didn't ask him to leave — they would work together as a couple, and he wanted that desperately.

He wasn't sure Jess could give him that, though.

Jess rubbed his face. "Are you sure you don't feel like this just because you're grateful?"

It took Bryce a second to understand what he was talking about. "You think I want to be with you because I'm grateful that you gave me a place to stay?" Bryce wasn't offended, even though he probably should be. He understood where Jess was coming from.

Jess shrugged. He avoided looking at Bryce when he answered. "I don't know. Right now, I don't know anything. I haven't felt this way in so long, and I can't help but wonder if I should trust my feelings."

At least he had feelings for Bryce. That was a good thing. "You're right. I *am* grateful for what you did. I would still be on the streets if you hadn't given me your guest room. But that's not why I like you. That's not why I'm falling in love with you." The words terrified Bryce, but he had to say them. He knew that was the only way Jess would believe him.

Jess' eyes widened. "You're falling in love with me?"

That wasn't the reaction Bryce had hoped for, but the words were out, and Bryce had to go on. "I am. And I'm not asking for you to do the same. I'm just telling you how I feel so that you know. I'll still leave once I find a job if that's what you want. Or I can go now. You don't owe me anything, not even your guest room."

"I don't want you to leave." Jess took Bryce's hand again, and Bryce allowed himself to breathe easier. It wasn't what he wanted to hear, not yet, but it was close. "I don't want you to go, not even when you find a job." Jess swallowed. "I never want you to leave, and I know it's too soon. That's what everyone will say."

"Does it matter, though? It might be soon, but as long as you and I feel the same way, I don't see why we should stay away from each other. What will that achieve? We'll both be frustrated and angry, and that's not going to help. So yes. I'm falling in love with you, and I love Taylor and living here. I don't want that to change."

Jess shook his head. "I don't want that to change either."

Bryce knew Jess was right. A lot of people would think that he was taking advantage of Jess, and maybe in a way, he was. He couldn't deny that thanks to Jess and Taylor, he had a roof over his head, warm food in his stomach every day, and yes, what seemed to be a little family. This was all Bryce had ever wanted in life, and he didn't want to lose it.

But that wasn't why he was falling in love with Jess. He was falling in love with Jess because Jess was a good man who'd offered someone he didn't know his guest room, even though Bryce could have been a serial killer. He was a man who hadn't freaked out when he'd found out that shifters were real. He was a man who listened to what Bryce had to say, and when he'd needed help, he'd reached out to Bryce because he knew Bryce was the one who could give him and Taylor answers.

Jess was a good man. *That* was why Bryce was falling in love with him.

Bryce wasn't sure what else he could tell Jess, though. He'd poured his heart out, and now Jess needed to take the next step.

And he did. Bryce yelped when Jess pulled on his hand, and he tilted forward in the armchair. He thought he was going to slam his face on the floor—and it wouldn't even be the first time in front of Jess—but instead, Jess pulled him closer.

Bryce tumbled on top of Jess, and both of them ended up spread out on the couch. Bryce looked down, wondering what was happening, but Jess was already moving again, hooking an arm around Bryce's neck and pulling him down until their lips met.

It was the first time they kissed, and Bryce would never forget it. It was everything he could have wanted or imagined, even though there was a little too much teeth. The kiss was frantic in the beginning, but once it slowed down, it was easier for Bryce to sink into it, to let Jess take his weight without thinking that he was too heavy.

Jess' hands buried into Bryce's hair, and he held him close as they kissed. Bryce wasn't sure where to put *his* hands. He was almost afraid to touch Jess, as if Jess might disappear if he did.

But Jess didn't.

Instead, he stopped kissing Bryce, and with eyes that glittered with pleasure and lust, he asked, "We should take this upstairs, don't you think?"

Bryce blinked a few times. His thoughts felt sluggish, but he needed to think. "Right. Taylor."

"Yes. Not that I care if he finds out we're together. You heard him. He wouldn't mind if we were boyfriends. But I don't want him to walk in on us having sex."

Bryce's mouth went dry. "We're going to have sex?"

Jess laughed. He sounded relieved, lighter, and Bryce felt smug at the thought that he'd been the one to do that. "That's what I was hoping, but we don't have to if you don't want to. I know we're rushing into this. We should probably take time to talk things out and date."

But Bryce didn't want that. He didn't care if they were rushing, because he wanted more.

He scrambled off the couch, almost falling on the coffee table, and held a hand out. "It's not too soon. Let's go to your bedroom." They would have to make sure to lock it, just in case, but Bryce couldn't wait.

Jess took his hand and got to his feet, and together, they turned off all the lights downstairs, made sure the doors were locked, then headed upstairs.

Bryce was nervous. He didn't have a lot of experience. The little he did have had been with people he didn't care about, not as much as he cared for Jess. He was terrified he was going to fuck things up, and he prayed he wouldn't. Jess was his future, and he needed to keep him close, but he wasn't sure how to make that happen.

"You're nervous," Jess said as they entered his bedroom.

Bryce knew the room, of course. Since he'd started taking care of the chores when he moved in with Jess and Taylor, he'd been in all the rooms, cleaning and putting things away. It was the first time he'd been in Jess's room for this reason, though, and yes, he was nervous. "A little."

Jess closed and locked the door, then reached for Bryce again. "I'm nervous, too. It's been a while for me."

Bryce sank into Jess' embrace, rubbing his cheek against Jess' chest. "Well, what you said to me downstairs goes for you, too. We don't have to do anything you're not comfortable doing."

"I'm not sure what I'm comfortable doing, but I can't wait to get you naked." He paused, and his chuckle made his chest vibrated. "Again."

Bryce's cheeks flushed as he remembered the first time Jess had seen him naked. He'd even fallen to his knees in front of him, exposing himself entirely. "That's what did it for you, isn't it?" he asked with laughter in his voice. Sex shouldn't be this fun, but with Jess, it was.

Even though they hadn't started yet.

"I don't think I'll ever forget that, no. But it's not what did it for me. Well, not entirely. I can't deny I find you gorgeous and that I can't wait to have you in my bed. But it's more than that. You're such a gentle and loving man. How could I not want you in my life?"

Bryce didn't know, but his nest certainly hadn't wanted him. He didn't want to think about them tonight, though, so he reached up and kiss Jess again.

Together, they tumbled onto the bed. Their clothes didn't stay on them for long, and even though Bryce was self-conscious about his body after being told he was fat so many times, he forced himself not to hide. He was done hiding. He was starting this new life with his chin raised high because he deserved it. He deserved *all* of this.

"You're gorgeous. I'll tell you until you believe me," Jess said as he ran his hands over Bryce's body. He settled on top of him, and Bryce opened his legs, wrapping himself around Jess. This was his life now. It would be his life forever, and he couldn't wait.

"I want you so much," Jess murmured as he kissed Bryce's neck.

Then there were no words anymore. Bryce focused on the way he and Jess moved together, on the pleasure building in his groin. He wanted so much more, but he knew it was too soon, and they had so many years waiting for them in which they could do this. There was no need for them to rush into anything. They would take their time, and it would be perfect.

And even though they only rubbed against each other, it *was* perfect. Bryce wouldn't have it any other way, even though he came embarrassingly fast. Jess didn't seem to care anyway. He continued moving on top of Bryce, kissing every inch of skin he could reach until he came, too.

Then Jess rolled off him and gathered him into his arms. They both smelled of sex and were sticky and sweaty, but Bryce couldn't remember a time in which he'd been happier and more relaxed.

He couldn't wait to see what the future would bring.

CHAPTER SEVEN

They were back at the shelter, and Jess couldn't help but think about when they'd adopted Bryce. Even though Bryce wasn't a rabbit, he wasn't going anywhere. He was part of Jess and Taylor's family now, and Jess couldn't have been happier.

Some days, he was still hesitant about all of this. He knew that some people thought he was crazy, moving in his boyfriend already, but they didn't know everything. They didn't know how he and Bryce had met. They didn't know what they talked about, what they did when they were together.

It felt right. That was the reason Jess wasn't freaking out over it more than he was. Just like being with Sandra had felt right, this did, too. He trusted Bryce. He knew that Bryce wasn't sticking around only because it was the best thing for him. He'd found a job, and it would have been easy for him to find an apartment now that he was earning money, but instead, he'd shown no indication that he wanted to leave, and Jess hadn't asked. He didn't want to make it happen by doing so.

It was something he and Bryce needed to talk about, but today was more important. Today, they were at the shelter with Taylor to pick another pet rabbit.

The thought made Jess smile. He could easily believe Taylor wanted another rabbit after he'd lost Thumper, but he hadn't thought that Bryce would agree. Instead, he thought it was a good idea, so here they were.

Taylor walked ahead while Bryce and Jess followed him.

Bryce leaned against Jess, and Jess wrapped an arm around his shoulders, kissing his temple. "You're okay?" he asked because he knew that Bryce didn't have many good memories of this place. He might not have been here long, but it couldn't have been easy for him.

"I'm fine. It's a little weird, but at least I'm not in a box this time."

Jess chuckled. "And you're never going to be in a box again." It was still strange to see Bryce shift sometimes or to go up to his bedroom and find a rabbit sleeping on his pillow, but Jess thought it was adorable. Besides, Bryce was as clean as a human being when he was in his rabbit form, and that was great. Jess didn't have to worry about finding poop under his blankets.

"What's going on in that head of yours?" Bryce asked.

He could read Jess better than anyone else sometimes. "Nothing."

"That's a lie, and we both know it. You don't have to tell me if you don't want to."

Jess shook his head and kissed Bryce again. "I'm just feeling a bit weird. Now that you found a job, we'll have to get used to a new routine."

"And you're afraid I'm going to leave."

Jess wasn't surprised Bryce had guessed. "Maybe a little bit."

"You don't have to be. Unless you and Taylor ask me to, I'm not going anywhere. You're stuck with me."

Jess chuckled, feeling lighter. "And I'm more than happy to be stuck with you." He wanted to kiss Bryce again, to drag him home and show him just how happy he was, but Taylor was waiting for him at the shelter door, hopping on his feet, excited about getting another pet. He rolled his eyes when they kissed, but thankfully, he didn't say anything.

He'd accepted Bryce and Jess' relationship easily enough.

Jess still thought that he found Bryce more interesting because he was a shifter than because he was his father's boyfriend, but that was okay. He treated Bryce with respect, and he listened to him as if he were another parent, even though he wasn't. Bryce would never try to replace Taylor's mother. He could be another father, though, and that was what they were working toward.

"Come on," he whined as Jess and Bryce finally reached him.

Jess couldn't help but smile. He felt like he'd been smiling the entire time since Bryce had hopped into his and Taylor's life, and he knew that wouldn't change. There would be hard times for the three of them. There would be fights, yelling, and disappointment. But they were a family, and they would stick together, always.

Jess was sure of that, and nothing would change his mind. He didn't care how long he and Bryce had been together or what anyone thought about their relationship. He wasn't giving Bryce up, and he knew that Taylor wouldn't, either.

That was all that mattered.

Bryce could tell Taylor was nervous by the way he bounced around, and he wasn't sure what was happening. Taylor shouldn't be nervous. He should be excited at the thought of getting another pet, and he was. But that nervousness was still worrying Bryce, and while Jess talked to Mark—AKA, the man who'd taken Bryce to the vet—Bryce moved closer to Taylor. "Everything okay?" he asked.

Taylor looked around, then leaned closer, and Bryce knew that he didn't want anyone to hear what he had to say. "What if I pick another shifter?"

So that was what worried him. "I doubt that's going to happen. You know I was here only because someone found me in the park."

"Maybe. But you *can't* promise it never happens. What if another rabbit shifter was found?"

Bryce crouched next to Taylor so he could look him in the eyes. "How about I promise you I'll help you choose your rabbit? I can make sure that none of them is a shifter. That way, you'll be able to pick whatever one you prefer." Bryce highly doubted the shelter had other shifters. He'd been unlucky, or maybe lucky considering how things had gone.

Being caught, spending time here, even if it had only been one day, hadn't been easy. He still had nightmares of cages, of getting kicked out, of being alone.

But he wasn't. He had Jess and Taylor, and he knew that if he played his cards right, he would always have them. The three of them were already a family, and they were settling in as one. Taylor hadn't said anything about Bryce and Jess being together, and Bryce didn't think he cared. He wanted Bryce around, and only that mattered to him.

Taylor nodded. "You can tell if any of them are shifters?"

"Sure. I told you shifters' sense of smell is much better than humans', right?"

"So you'll be able to smell if any of the rabbits are shifters."

"Exactly."

"Ready to go?" Jess asked from behind them.

Bryce got to his feet and smiled at him. "We were just talking about what kind of rabbit Taylor might want."

"What did you say happened to the other one?" Mark asked.

Bryce couldn't help but glare at him, and Mark blinked, no doubt wondering what he'd done to earn that.

Bryce wasn't about to tell him, of course, but he forced himself to smile. "Nothing. But we thought that it could use a friend."

"Oh, sure. It was a boy, right? So you probably want to

avoid a girl so they don't reproduce."

"Don't worry about that. I know how to take care of rabbits."

The man blinked again, but Bryce focused on Taylor. He held his hand out, and even though Taylor was eight and was usually more than happy to walk on his own, he took Bryce's hand, and together, they followed Mark outside.

Bryce remembered this place, but it didn't give him bad memories right now. If anything, it reminded him of when Jess and Taylor had chosen him, of when they'd taken him home. Some days, he still had a hard time believing that Taylor had picked a rabbit that looked like he could kill him in his sleep, but he was happy. He wouldn't change what had happened for anything, even though it had been hard, and it still was, sometimes.

Taylor let go of Bryce's hand and made a beeline for the enclosure with the rabbits hopping inside. Bryce followed, and even though it took a while for him to be sure, he could confirm that none of the rabbits were shifters. Once Taylor knew that he looked more excited, and he started talking to Mark about the bunnies' personalities. Bryce took a step back, giving Taylor the space he needed to choose his pet, and moved closer to Jess, who wrapped his arm around Bryce again.

He always did that, and Bryce loved it.

"What was that about?" Jess asked.

"He was worried he'd pick another shifter."

Jess muffled a laugh. "Of course he was. What did you tell him?"

"That they're all normal rabbits. And don't laugh. It's kind of adorable."

"You're right, it is. I'm happy he has you to ask that kind of question."

Bryce grinned. "And I'm happy he'll have you to have the

sex talk with once it's time for it."

Jess paled, and Bryce laughed again. Jess took a step away from him, moving toward Taylor, no doubt thinking that his little boy was too young for such a talk. He was right, but it wouldn't be long, just a few years.

And Bryce would be there to see it. This was his life now, his family. He'd been so sad and desperate when he'd been kicked out, and he thought he would never have this. He'd thought his life was over, but instead, he'd found his way to Jess and Taylor. Together, they were hopping to happiness, and Bryce wouldn't have it any other way.

Noel
Catherine Lievens

Excerpt

Roark wanted to throttle Noel. How could he say being mates wasn't important and that he didn't care?

But that wasn't what he was saying, not exactly.

Roark opened his mouth, but Kameron beat him to it. "Do I have to separate the two of you? Because the last thing I want is to have to break up a fight. I do enough of that with the twins."

Roark gritted his teeth. Kameron was his boss, or one of them anyway. He needed to stop acting like a fucking moron and show him and the council he knew how to do his job, even if it meant playing babysitter to his mate—a mate who didn't seem to want him.

He couldn't blame Noel for leaving that night, just like he couldn't blame him for being defensive now. He could probably tell how fucked-up Roark was just by looking at him, or maybe through the bond.

Because there was a bond between them. Roark could feel it. He'd always been able to feel it, and he'd clung to it through the pain and torture. It had never completely disappeared, but its presence had softened to the point that Roark managed to ignore it most days. But Noel was in front of him now. He should have realized something was wrong as soon as he'd been shimmered into the apartment, but he'd been focused on Kameron and the job. The flare of the bond was pretty obvious, though, and there was no way he was going to be able to ignore it, but he was going to do his damn best.

"We're okay," he said, his voice hard.

He had to be hard if he wanted to survive the job and the time spent with Noel. He could break down once he was back home, but not before. Not in front of Noel.

Kameron arched a brow. "You sure? Because you don't look like you are. You look pissed."

"I always look pissed. I wouldn't be a council assassin if I was always smiling and skipping in a meadow full of fucking wildflowers."

"That's surprisingly detailed," Kameron said.

Roark shrugged and looked at Noel. How was he reacting to the news of what Roark was? Roark expected fear, maybe disgust, but Noel was staring at him with a thoughtful expression on his face. Roark couldn't read him, and he didn't want to. He couldn't allow himself to want anything, not when it came to Noel. He was going home once the asshole threatening Noel was caught, and he was going alone. Noel had his life, and from the look of his apartment, it was a good one. He wouldn't want anything to do with a fucked-up killer, and even if by some miracle he did, Roark wouldn't allow him to ruin his life that way.

He might be angry at Noel, but that didn't mean he wanted to fuck him up.

"As long as both of you are sure you're not going to try to murder each other, I don't see any problem in Roark protecting you, Noel," Kameron said.

"You don't?"

"No."

"I thought bodyguards weren't supposed to fall for their clients because they might lose objectivity or something," Noel offered

"Who said I was going to fall in love with you?" Roark asked, trying to sound amused.

He wasn't sure he managed, because he knew how this was going to end. He was going to spend days, if not weeks, with Noel, and he was going to fall in love with him. Leaving was going to hurt like a bitch, but Roark would do it. In the meantime, there was no way he was putting his mate's life into someone else's hands, no matter what he'd said, and Kameron knew it.

"You're an asshole," Noel snapped.

"Never claimed otherwise."

"Children," Kameron scolded. He didn't look angry, but Roark knew better than to push him. He'd heard what happened when the man got angry, and it never ended well.

He pressed his lips together and stared at Kameron so he wouldn't have to look at Noel, but Noel's image was seared into his mind.

His mate had aged well. He'd been gorgeous at nineteen, but he looked incredible at thirty-six.

He was more beautiful, more mature and settled. His blond hair was slightly darker and was cut in a current style. His blue eyes still glittered, although at the moment it was from anger rather than lust and pleasure. He had small laugh lines around them, showing he wasn't as young as he looked, especially in his pajamas. He'd filled out, his shoulders larger, his arms stronger, and Roark wondered what he looked like under the soft, formless clothes he wore.

He wasn't going to find out, no matter how much he wanted to.

"I'll make the rounds," Roark said.

Kameron nodded. Roark left Noel and Kameron in the living room and went to explore what was going to be his home for at least a few weeks. The apartment wasn't large, and from what he saw, Noel lived alone. He hadn't realized how frightened he was that Noel had found someone until he realized he hadn't.

It would have made sense. Noel was thirty-six, more than old enough to have a husband, a family. But there were no pictures of Noel with anyone on the walls or in the bedroom. The only thing hanging on the wall was art, and while Roark didn't understand much about it, he liked the displayed photographs and paintings.

The master bedroom and bathroom looked lived in, but they were neat and clean. The guest room temperature was cool, the bed perfectly made, not one personal object in sight. The kitchen and living room space, too, looked like it wasn't used much, which didn't surprise Roark. He didn't know a lot about Noel, but from the way Kameron talked about him, he was a good lawyer. That had to mean long hours and not a lot of time home.

The apartment wouldn't be hard to defend. The only point of entry was the front door, because there was no way anyone could climb the eight floors unless they were some kind of bird shifter. From what Roark knew, he doubted a shifter was behind this, though. It sounded more like some human was pissed that Noel tried to help shifters. It wasn't anything new. Still, Roark made sure the windows and the door leading from the kitchen to the tiny balcony were locked. The kitchen and the living room were one big open space, and it would be easy to control.

Noel and Kameron were still in the living room when he looked at them, their heads close together. He hovered by the kitchen counter, unsure what to do. He hated feeling off-center, and that was exactly how he felt at that moment. He didn't know how to deal with Noel. He wanted to throw him on the couch like his bear was pushing him to do, but he couldn't. He also couldn't talk, not in front of Kameron, not with what might come out of his mouth. The last thing he wanted was to make himself vulnerable by telling Noel about his past and his feelings.

No way was that happening. Nope.

Kameron finally looked up when one of the women Roark had seen in the entrance walked into the room and cleared her throat.

"We're done, Alpha Rhett."

Kameron nodded. "Good. You can leave whenever you find someone to shimmer you. Call Bran if no one is available."

She nodded and walked away, and Kameron looked at Noel again. "I'll send someone to clean the wall tomorrow."

"You don't need to do that."

"Maybe not, but I want to. I'll take care of it while you're at work. You should go to bed and rest. Don't worry about anything. We've got you covered." Kameron looked at Roark. "Well, he's got you covered. I'm out of here. The twins were going to wait for me to have ice cream, and they're going to eat the entire container if I don't hurry."

Noel laughed. The sound made Roark's skin tingle. He remembered that sound, although it had been huskier seventeen years ago—but then, the situation had been wholly different.

He couldn't let himself think about Noel in bed, though, not if he wanted to survive the next few weeks. Once Noel was safe and Roark was home, he'd let himself think about what he'd lost. Not one moment before, though. He couldn't afford to lose his focus, or Noel would pay the price.

ABOUT THE AUTHOR

Catherine is the creator of several series, most of them paranormal, including the Whitedell Pride Series and the Gillham Pack Series. While she graduated in translation, she decided to go the writer's way because it was more fun to create her own stories and characters.

She's been living in Italy for more than twenty years, but she's a daughter of the North—Belgium to be precise—and she misses it so much that she's already planning to move back.

She loves pizza—probably too much—her pets, and of course, books. She sneaks some reading time in her schedule every time she has five minutes free from writing, demands from her various pets and son, and lastly, housework.

Connect with her:

lievens.catherine@gmail.com
BookBub
Website
Facebook
Facebook Group
Twitter
Newsletter